JoJo's Jump

Dedicated to my precious daughter, Romy, and to all children everywhere, each of whom have the power inside them to accomplish extraordinary things out of ordinary circumstances; with self-belief and a positive mindset, there is nothing you cannot do. – **S.M.**

For my equestrian-loving daughters. – **N.M.**

Published in Great Britain in 2022
by Little Steps Publishing
Uncommon, 126 New King's Rd, London SW6 4LZ
www.littlestepspublishing.co.uk

ISBN: 978-1-912678-48-8

A CIP catalogue record for this book is available from the British Library.

Designed by Rachel Lawston

Printed in China

10 9 8 7 6 5 4 3 2 1

JoJo's Jump

Written by
Stephanie Mason

Illustrated by
Natalie Merheb

Little Steps
PUBLISHING

Inside the stable and fast asleep,
Was the happiest pony you ever did meet.

With a soft chestnut coat and a long golden tail,
Looking her best, she never did fail.

JoJo they called her, that was her name.
There was no pony like her, not one the same.

Sweet little JoJo had grown up on the farm,
Grazing in fields amongst the country charm.

Some time had passed and the pony had grown,
It was time for her to come into her own.

So down to the field the pony was led,
Not just for grazing but training instead!

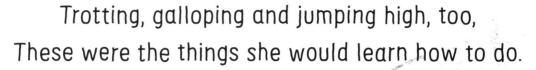

Trotting, galloping and jumping high, too,
These were the things she would learn how to do.

Out in the fields was a jump standing high,
JoJo knew this was her moment to try.

The pony felt nervous; a little bit wary,
This whole jumping thing was almost too scary.
Now was the time to be put through her paces,
And then, just like that, she saw kind, friendly faces.

All of her friends had rallied around,
Coming to support her from down on the ground.

There was Bob the bunny, all fluffy and white,
Who cheered on the pony with all of his might.

With Fiona the frog and the sheep they called Peggy,
They gathered together united already.

They knew she could do it although this was new,
Deep down the pony would know what to do.

And with her friends' support, she began to decide,
That this jump was something she would take in her stride.
She cantered along, her hooves moving fast,
This may be her first jump but would not be her last.

GO JOJO

She wanted to fly right over the top,
But, all of a sudden, there was **a loud FLOP!**

JoJo had missed and had now fallen down,
What could be seen? Oh no, a small frown!

Don't worry, smiled Bob, this was your first try,
Remember it takes time to reach for the sky.
We know you can do it, this much is true,
Believe in yourself as we believe in you!

JoJo thanked her friends and another go she gave,
The sheep and the frog thought her to be brave.

She raced to the jump and then over she flew,

With a positive attitude, there is nothing you can't do!

Her hooves hit the ground and friends gave a cheer,
This brave little pony had nothing to fear.

Back in her stable eating heaps of hay,
JoJo's friends all talked of her special day.

This courageous pony was growing up fast,
This new-found skill would not be her last.

But for now she was sleepy, it was soon to be night,
Already outside there was soft, fading light.

A new day tomorrow with plenty of fun,
More things to accomplish out in the sun.
Her friends said good night and went off to bed,
For they knew JoJo had a bright future ahead.